ANATOLE

and

the Cat

OLE
and the Cat

by Eve Titus
Pictures by Paul Galdone

A BANTAM LITTLE ROOSTER BOOK
NEW YORK · TORONTO · LONDON · SYDNEY · AUCKLAND

For Joanna and Ferencz Galdone
and my son Richard, too

ANATOLE AND THE CAT
*A Bantam Little Rooster Book / published by arrangement with
the author and illustrator's estate*

PRINTING HISTORY
McGraw-Hill edition published 1956
*Special thanks to the Kerlan Collection at the University of Minnesota for
making original illustration materials available to us.*
*Little Rooster is a trademark of Bantam Books, a division of Bantam
Doubleday Dell Publishing Group, Inc.*
Bantam edition/July 1990

Library of Congress Cataloging-in-Publication Data
Titus, Eve.
   Anatole and the cat / by Eve Titus; illustrated by Paul Galdone.
—Bantam.
   p. cm.
   "A Bantam Little Rooster book."
   Summary: Anatole's job as a taster in a cheese factory is
endangered by a marauding cat.
   ISBN 0-553-34871-X
   [1. Mice—Fiction. 2. Cats—Fiction.] I. Galdone, Paul, ill.
II. Title.
PZ7.T543Am 1990
[E]—dc20   89-17590
                                                              CIP
                                                               AC

Published simultaneously in the United States and Canada

Bantam Books are published by Bantam Books, a division of Bantam
Doubleday Dell Publishing Group, Inc. Its trademark, consisting of
the words "Bantam Books" and the portrayal of a rooster, is Registered
in U.S. Patent and Trademark Office and in other countries. Marca
Registrada. Bantam Books, 666 Fifth Avenue, New York, New York
10103.

PRINTED IN THE UNITED STATES OF AMERICA

0 9 8 7 6 5 4 3 2 1

In all France
there was no mouse more honored or respected
than Anatole.

He was very proud of his job as Cheese Taster
at the factory of M'sieu Duval.

Nobody knew that he was not a man but a mouse,
not even M'sieu Duval,
for he did his work after the others went home.

Always his dear wife Doucette blew him a kiss
as he left the mouse village
and bicycled off to Paris on business,

after their six charming children were sound asleep.

One night Anatole entered the Cheese-Tasting Room
with Gaston, his good friend and helper.

Anatole tasted some Brie and made a face. "Too salty!
Give me a NOT SO GOOD sign, and I'll write it down."

Just then they heard soft footsteps on the floor above.
They began to shiver and shake and quiver and quake!
"IT IS A CAT!" cried Anatole. "Still, we must do our job.
As long as he stays upstairs—we work.
As soon as he starts downstairs—out the window we go!"

They did their best, but they were much too frightened!
Gaston kept dropping signs on the floor.
And Anatole scribbled just anything that came into his head!

"Alas, I fear I have made some serious mistakes," he said.
"But it's all the fault of that awful animal—
to be a cat is to be a monster and a menace!"

Then they ran for the window—the cat was on the stairs!
They climbed down in a big hurry
and bicycled home at about a mile a minute!

That night millions of cats marched through Anatole's dreams,
shouting, "Down with Anatole! Down with Anatole!"

At dawn, when the sky turned pale pink,
he left his bed, as miserable as a mouse could be.

10

At breakfast he could scarcely swallow his food.

The children were upset to see him looking so sad.
"What is worrying our dearest *Papa?*" they asked anxiously.

But Anatole felt they were still too young to learn about cats,
and he hurried them off to school.

Then he hung his head in the deepest despair.
"Doucette, there was a You-Know-What at the factory!"

She turned pale. "*Quelle horreur!* What will you do?"

"It is with such pride that I earn my family's bread and cheese, instead of stooping to take people's scraps.
Must I change my honorable way of life because of this beast?"

But Doucette said, "No cat has appeared there before.
Perhaps this one came out of curiosity, and will never return."

Anatole hugged her. "You give me new hope, *ma petite*.
How would I manage without such a jewel of a wife?"

And he ate his breakfast, for now he had an appetite.

At that very moment the factory was in a hullabaloo!
The cheese workers were quarreling like cats and dogs!

Half of them shouted that they must do what the signs said—
the other half screamed that the signs were full of mistakes!

They sent for M'sieu Duval, the president of the factory.
He came at once, with a large cat perched upon his shoulder.

"*Regardez!*" they cried, pointing to the signs.

GOOD
needs melted
chocolate Anatole

EXTRA-'SPECIALLY
GOOD
throw it in the
garbage pail!
Anatole

FROMAGE

NOT SO GOOD
use frogs' legs
Anatole

NO GOOD
but use six
moldy marshmallows
Anatole

'SPECIALLY
GOOD
add some pickled
strawberries Anatole

M'sieu Duval scratched his head, greatly puzzled.

"What strange signs! I trust Anatole as I would trust myself—
has he not made our cheeses the finest in all France?
Still, it does seem odd to wrap cheese in a banana peel.
And who ever heard of using chopped cucumber seeds?
Can it be that he has invented some brand-new cheeses?
Or has Anatole been working too hard?
I shall send him a memo, inquiring as to his health.
Meanwhile, Men, do just what the signs order you to do!"

14

And he left the room, patting his cat, and saying,
"You did not come home last night. Where were you, *mon ami?*"

The cat purred and blinked his bright green eyes.

When Anatole tooted his horn for Gaston that night,
his friend appeared at the window, holding a little bell.

"I am a mouse of caution, I do not wish to live dangerously.
You must work alone at the factory after this—
mouse-eating monsters are not for me!"

Then he tinkled the bell. "Of course, if you can bell the cat—"

"Make no jokes about such a serious matter! *Au 'voir!*"

Squeezing under the factory door,
Anatole listened for cat sounds, but happily there were none.

In the Tasting Room he found a short memo from M'sieu Duval,
asking him whether he felt quite right,
and begging him to take a holiday if he needed one.

He went to M'sieu Duval's office and typed a memo in reply.

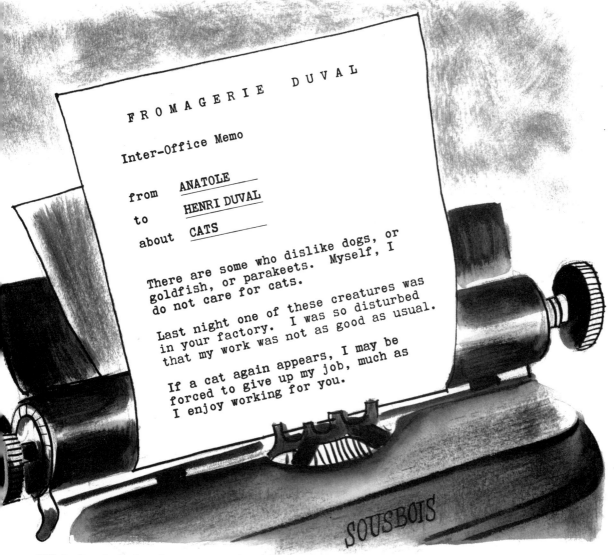

FROMAGERIE DUVAL

Inter-Office Memo

from   ANATOLE

to   HENRI DUVAL

about   CATS

There are some who dislike dogs, or
goldfish, or parakeets. Myself, I
do not care for cats.

Last night one of these creatures was
in your factory. I was so disturbed
that my work was not as good as usual.

If a cat again appears, I may be
forced to give up my job, much as
I enjoy working for you.

This he left in the typewriter.
"Now we shall see what we shall see!"

The next night there was a second memo from M'sieu Duval in reply to the memo from Anatole.

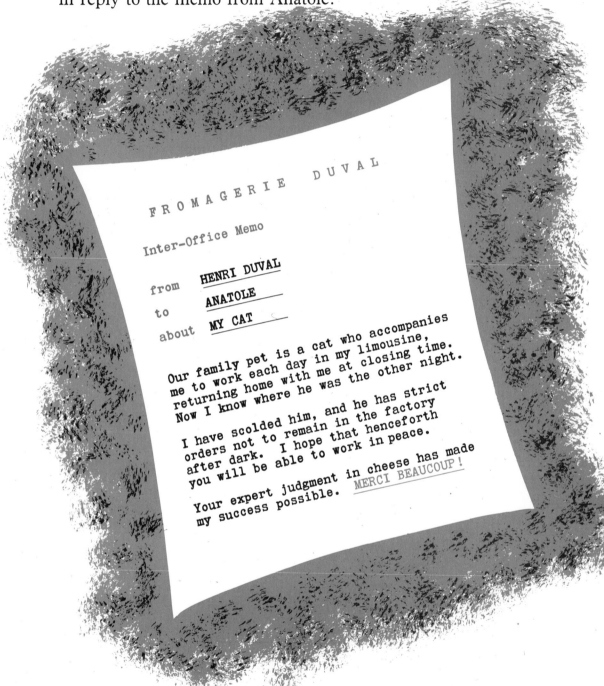

FROMAGERIE DUVAL

Inter-Office Memo

from HENRI DUVAL

to ANATOLE

about MY CAT

Our family pet is a cat who accompanies me to work each day in my limousine, returning home with me at closing time. Now I know where he was the other night.

I have scolded him, and he has strict orders not to remain in the factory after dark. I hope that henceforth you will be able to work in peace.

Your expert judgment in cheese has made my success possible. MERCI BEAUCOUP!

At first Anatole rejoiced. "My worries are at an end! This cat loves M'sieu Duval and will surely obey him." But then he asked himself—is a cat to be trusted? 18   And the answer was—*Non!*

At home he sat silent, staring at the slanting rain,
remembering Gaston's joke, and a tale known the world over—

Long, long ago many mice had met to decide what to do about a cat.
Someone had the idea of putting a bell around its neck.
This would warn them of its coming, and all were pleased
until a wise old mouse said, "But *who* will bell the cat?"

Not one mouse had dared to do it, then or ever!

There must be a way, thought Anatole, pacing up and down.

For hours and hours his brain was busy with ideas,
but they all seemed too dangerous until he suddenly remembered
a big empty crate in the storeroom of the factory.

And Anatole smiled, for now he had the perfect plan!

Before leaving, he asked Doucette for her sash.
She was worried. "Has it anything to do with the cat, *chéri?*
Be careful—not all the cheese in France could replace you!"
Anatole kissed her good-bye, telling her nothing.

He stopped off at Gaston's and asked for the bell.
Gaston guessed the reason. "Do not risk your life, I beg of you!"

But Anatole began stringing the sash through the top of the bell.
"The brute will be there tonight—I feel it in my bones!"

On the way to work, Anatole entered a pet shop.
He took a box of catnip,
leaving some Camembert cheese in payment.

Then he went to a hardware shop.
There he took a door latch,
leaving some Roquefort cheese in payment.

Arrived at the factory, he typed a memo in M'sieu Duval's office.
He hurried to the storeroom, where he tried the door of the crate.
It swung to and fro easily, and he hammered the latch into place.
Then he put the catnip in the crate, at the far end.

"*Voilà!* If a man may build a mouse-trap,
then a mouse may build a cat-trap!"

He hid himself and waited. Soon his sharp ears heard sounds—
was it the cat, or was it the thumping of his own heart?

IT WAS THE CAT! Smelling the catnip, he bounded into the crate!

Quick as a wink Anatole slammed the door,
scurried up and latched the latch, and scurried down.

The angry cat tried and tried, but the door would not open.
"How dare you trap me!" he raged. "My name is Charlemagne,
and I come from a long line of illustrious cats.
My great-great-great-great-great-great-great-great grandfather
was the pet of the Emperor Charlemagne himself. LET ME OUT!"

Anatole spoke softly.
"My dear Charlemagne,
what about the catnip?"

"I'll gobble it up!
And then, beware—
you little nobody of a mouse!"

But when the catnip was gone,
Charlemagne completely forgot
about Anatole!

He grinned and began to do
all sorts of silly things—
chasing his tail,
turning somersaults,
trying to stand on his head,
and prancing and dancing
wildly around the crate!

Anatole waited patiently,
not a bit surprised—
he knew catnip did this to cats.

At last Charlemagne grew tired,
and stretched out and slept.

thought Anatole—a sleeping cat cannot pounce!
snores were like the rumble of thunder,
nouse did what had to be done,
g bow when he saw the sash was too long.

Then he taped the memo to the crate and went upstairs.
To celebrate, he fixed himself a special treat—
a triple-decker sandwich with six different kinds of cheese!

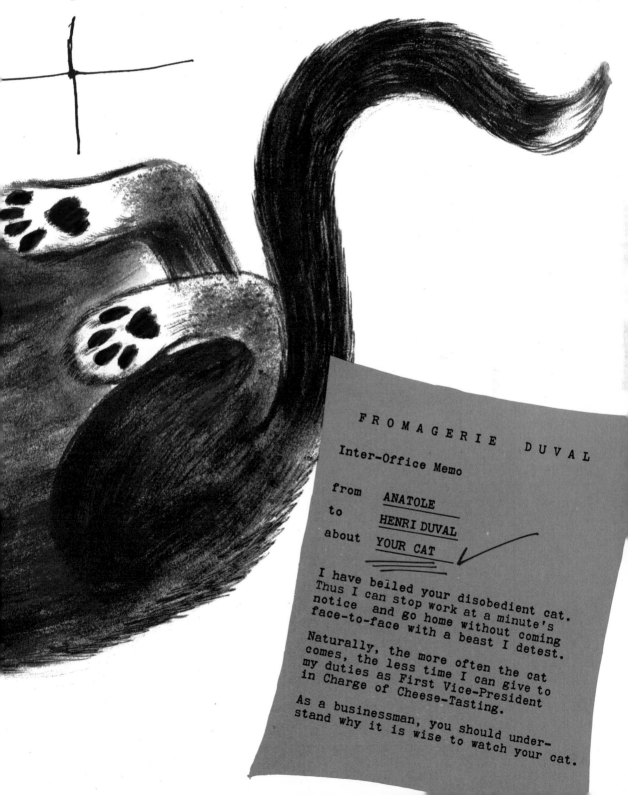

FROMAGERIE DUVAL

Inter-Office Memo

from   ANATOLE

to   HENRI DUVAL

about   YOUR CAT

I have boiled your disobedient cat.
Thus I can stop work at a minute's
notice and go home without coming
face-to-face with a beast I detest.

Naturally, the more often the cat
comes, the less time I can give to
my duties as First Vice-President
in Charge of Cheese-Tasting.

As a businessman, you should under-
stand why it is wise to watch your cat.

Upon hearing the news, Gaston gladly returned to work.
Sometimes they were bothered by the tinkling of the bell.
But M'sieu Duval kept close watch on Charlemagne,
and this happened only once in a while.

When it did, the two friends dashed madly for the window,
and climbed down as fast as their legs would let them!

One Friday night Anatole took his family to see the factory.
Bicycling along the boulevard toward Paris, the children said,
"*Papa,* did you think we were too young to be told about cats?
Our teacher taught us all about them."

That was the night the wonderful letter was waiting!

DUVAL
LE MEILLEUR FROMAGE DU MONDE

My dear Anatole,

Because of last month's mistakes, the people of France all had stomach aches! They demanded that I go out of business, but I begged for another chance. Since then your work has been so good that they have all taken the Duval cheeses back to their hearts--or should I say to their stomachs?

And now, my dear Vice-President, I have a surprise. On the night of the mistakes one sign said: ADD CHOPPED CUCUMBER SEEDS. This cucumber cheese is so tasty that it has become the people's favorite. Congratulations!

In your honor I have named it CHEESE ANATOLE!

Your friend,

P.S. Belling the cat was an excellent idea.

Henri Duval

Doucette was so pleased that she wept for joy.

Paul and Paulette,
Claude and Claudette,
and Georges and Georgette
all exclaimed proudly,
"Our *Papa* is so clever that a cheese has been named after him!"

And Gaston declared, "I said it before and I say it once more—
HE IS A MOUSE MAGNIFIQUE! VIVE ANATOLE!"

So Anatole again became
the most honored, respected mouse in all France.

And he was also the bravest, because—
for thousands of years
the mice of the world
had talked about belling the cat,
but Anatole
was the only one
who did it!